PROJECT GEMINI BOOKS

♊

PROJECT GEMINI IS A UNIQUE COLLECTION OF BOOKS AIMED AT GETTING THE EIGHT-TO-TEN-YEAR-OLD RELUCTANT READER EXCITED TO READ.

SOME CHILDREN STOP READING AFTER CHAPTER BOOKS BECAUSE THEY NEVER FEEL THAT EAGERNESS TO TURN THE PAGE. THE BOOKS IN THE PROJECT GEMINI SERIES WERE WRITTEN WITH THAT CHILD IN MIND.

PROJECT GEMINI IS A TEN-BOOK SERIES INVOLVING THE CHARACTERS PIRATE NINJA, LOVABLE LOSER, LUNCHMEAT LENNY, AND OLIVE KLEIN. THESE ARE DISTINCT CHARACTERS, EACH WITH THEIR OWN SEPARATE STORIES, BUT ALL THE STORIES EXIST WITHIN THE SAME FICTIONAL UNIVERSE.

THESE BOOKS ARE FUNNY AND FAST-PACED, MAKING THEM PERFECT FOR RELUCTANT READERS, AND THEY'RE CAREFULLY DESIGNED TO INCREASE VERY GRADUALLY IN DIFFICULTY, COMPLEXITY, AND LENGTH, HELPING YOUNG READERS GROW IN ABILITY AND CONFIDENCE AS THEY PROCEED.

IN BOOK TEN OF THE COLLECTION, THE MAIN CHARACTERS FROM THE PREVIOUS NINE BOOKS COME TOGETHER TO FORM "GEMINI SQUAD," AN ELITE GROUP OF KIDS RESPONSIBLE FOR FIGHTING THE FORCES OF EVIL. (YOU KNOW, THOSE FORCES OF EVIL THAT ADULTS ARE HELPLESS TO STOP ON THEIR OWN!)

LEARN MORE ABOUT PROJECT GEMINI AT WWW.DANIELKENNEY.COM.

PROJECT GEMINI BOOKS

BOOK ONE: PIRATE NINJA 1
BOOK TWO: LOVABLE LOSER 1
BOOK THREE: PIRATE NINJA 2
BOOK FOUR: LOVABLE LOSER 2
BOOK FIVE: PIRATE NINJA 3
BOOK SIX: PIRATE NINJA 4
BOOK SEVEN: LUNCHMEAT LENNY 1
BOOK EIGHT: LUNCHMEAT LENNY 2
BOOK NINE: THE UNBEATABLE OLIVE KLEIN
BOOK TEN: GEMINI SQUAD

ALSO BY DANIEL KENNEY

THE MATH INSPECTORS SERIES
THE SCIENCE INSPECTORS SERIES
THE HISTORY MYSTERY KIDS SERIES
THE BIG LIFE OF REMI MULDOON SERIES
TEENAGE TREASURE HUNTER
KATIE PLUMB & THE PENDLETON GANG
BUT, I STILL HAD FEET

PIRATE NINJA 3
HALLOWEEN HOOLIGANS

DANIEL KENNEY

♊

PROJECT GEMINI BOOK FIVE

TRENDWOOD PRESS

Cover: Author Support
Illustrations: Sumit Roy
Editing: David Gatewood
Formatting: Polgarus Studio

SIGN UP FOR THE NO-SPAM NEWSLETTER AND GET TWO STORIES PLUS ALWAYS BE THE FIRST TO KNOW ABOUT NEW CONTENT, ALL FOR FREE.

DETAILS CAN BE FOUND AT THE END OF THIS BOOK.

The following is a decrypted text message conversation between a secure location in Virginia and someplace in the northern Nevada desert.

DATE: October 26
SUBJECT: PROJECT GEMINI

BALTHASAR: This loser from Ohio is growing on me.

EVIE: What'd he do now, win a squirt gun battle?

BALTHASAR: Even better, he won a sledding contest.

EVIE: Wait. In October?

BALTHASAR: Ohio had an early snow.

EVIE: AND BECAUSE HE CAN SLED YOU WANT HIM TO BE ONE OF MY AGENTS?

BALTHASAR: YOU'RE NOT FOLLOWING. THE KID'S GOT MOXIE.

EVIE: MOXIE? I'M 25 YEARS OLD. I DON'T SPEAK OLD PERSON.

BALTHASAR: GRRR. THIS SEAN KELLY, HE RACED HIS SLED OVER A CREEK. JUMPED RIGHT OVER IT. HADN'T BEEN DONE IN THIRTY YEARS.

EVIE: CAN HE BUILD SNOWMEN TOO?

BALTHASAR: YOU'RE NOT LISTENING. AFTER HE JUMPED THE CREEK HE SAVED A GIRL FROM GETTING SMASHED BY ONCOMING TRAFFIC. THE KID'S GOT COURAGE, FIGHT. HE'S GOT MOXIE!

EVIE: OKAY.

BALTHASAR: OKAY YOU WANT TO KNOW MORE?

EVIE: OKAY, NOW I UNDERSTAND WHAT MOXIE IS.

BALTHASAR: HOW'S KNOFFLER?

EVIE: HE WANTS RESULTS. YESTERDAY.

BALTHASAR: YOU'LL FIGURE IT OUT.

EVIE: IT'S LIKE MAGELLAN'S ALWAYS ONE STEP AHEAD OF US.

BALTHASAR: LIKE I SAID, YOU'LL FIGURE IT OUT.

EVIE: HOW CAN YOU BE SO SURE?

BALTHASAR: EASY. YOU'VE GOT MOXIE. ☺

CHAPTER 1

My name is Archie Beller, and I am Pirate Ninja—though no one other than my crazy Superhero Coach, Grievous, knows that.

Not Kings Cove District Attorney Vincent, who secretly goes by the name "the Vulture" and runs a huge crime syndicate.

Not my mother, who makes beefy lasagna on Wednesday nights.

Not even my best friends, the Nimrods.

But after my last adventure, my friends *were*

starting to get suspicious. Heck, everyone was getting suspicious. I had embarrassed District Attorney Vincent so badly that he made it his life's mission to discover the true identity of Pirate Ninja. He convinced the local paper, *the Daily Cove*, to run a daily segment called "Who Is Pirate Ninja?"

So far, the newspaper had guessed that it might be anyone from Uncle Phil, the guy who ran the city's swimming pool, to Duffy the Dog, a three-legged golden retriever who happened to be the mascot of Kings Cove's semi-professional baseball team, The Kings Cove Ruff Ruffs. In other words, the newspaper had no idea—but they thought it would be fun to accuse random people each and every day.

And what did I do?

As had become my custom, on most nights I snuck out of my house and patrolled the rooftops of downtown Kings Cove, looking for trouble.

Ever since Grievous had gotten me a special zoom lens to hide inside my pirate patch, I'd developed super vision in my left eye. And so it was that three nights after saving my friend Freddie from the Vulture's clutches, I used my super vision to spot a woman four blocks away walking in the dark all by herself.

Immediately my Pirate Ninja senses went on high alert. And for good reason: a dirtball was thirty feet behind her. He was wearing a dark leather jacket, a black stocking cap, and carried himself like a tough guy. And he wasn't even trying to be sneaky. He came running down the alley right for this lady.

I immediately took off on a dead sprint across the rooftops. By now, I had become an expert at using the high-tech super boots Grievous had given me. They allowed me to bound from rooftop to rooftop with no problem. I jumped off the final rooftop, hit the ground thirty feet below like I'd just jumped off my couch, and rolled three times just as the thug grabbed the woman's purse. She screamed at the sight of him, then screamed again when she saw me.

But her crazy scream didn't distract me from the task at hand. I was used to having that effect on girls. I took my wooden sword and caught Mr. McThug in the back of the foot. That lifted him off his feet, and he slammed down onto his back.

But like I said, this guy was Grade A thug. So he leapt back up and started wildly throwing punches. Gotta hand it to him: he tried to put up a good fight.

The operative word being *tried*.

After missing with his first twenty punches, McThug charged me like an angry bull. He swung the kind of punch that would probably have separated my head from my body if it connected. But it didn't. I ducked, jabbed the wooden sword into his belly, then swept his legs with a well-executed back leg sweep. He fell hard on his side. I grabbed the woman's purse from him and held up my sword for one more swing.

The guy held his hands up to his face and begged, "Don't. Please don't. I'll leave. I swear. I'll never do anything like this ever again."

Then he started to cry.

For real.

Like, it was embarrassing. Worse, it was

pathetic. And apparently, it was also smart—because it made me relax just enough for McThug to jump to his feet and sprint away. I could have caught him, of course, but I wasn't in the mood.

I turned around and handed the woman her purse.

"Thank you, Pirate Ninja. I can't believe you're real."

"I can't believe I'm real either," I said in the Spanish Irish accent I'd been working on. I hadn't perfected my superhero chitchat yet, however. I was still working out the kinks.

I noticed a piece of blue paper on the ground. I picked it up and handed it over. "I think this must have fallen out of your purse."

She shook her head. "Must belong to that guy. You should give it to the police." She grabbed my arm and squeezed. "Thank you, Pirate Ninja, I'll never forget you."

My face got instantly hot, and I felt nervous.

But not too nervous for the perfect response.

"I'll never forget me either," I replied.

Like I said, still ironing out the superhero chitchat.

After the woman walked off, I examined that blue paper. There was writing on it, in black ink.

October 31.

That was Halloween. Two days away.

Below the date were six words:

Downtown. The Mother of All Jobs.

Finally, at the bottom, was a name. And not just any name.

The Vulture.

My heart quickened.

The Vulture was pulling the mother of all jobs on Halloween?

Not good. Not good at all.

That woman was right. I really should take this to the police. There was just one problem: the police weren't that happy about Pirate Ninja. District Attorney Vincent had them convinced

Pirate Ninja was a bad guy, despite all the good things I'd done. I thought about going to see Grievous to get his advice, but he was going to be out of town for a couple more days. It looked like I'd need to take care of this one solo.

The good news was, I doubted any more crimes would take place before Halloween.

Which was perfect, because I still needed to get my costume ready.

CHAPTER 2

Originally, Eduardo wanted us to go dressed up like Nimrods for Halloween.

Literally.

He wanted us to dress up as the different letters to spell the word "Nimrods." As you can tell, he's really proud of our name. I've told Eduardo repeatedly that Nimrods is actually an insult, but he disagrees. He continues to remind me that it's the name of a mighty warrior from the Bible. And the fact that McGinley, Barry, and the rest of them don't know that? According to Eduardo, that makes them the *real* nimrods.

He and I are going to have to disagree about that one.

Anyways, I managed to convince him that dressing as superheroes would be a lot more fun than dressing up as letters of the alphabet. You might think that would be an easy case to make, but with Eduardo, you never know.

We had all been brainstorming superhero ideas for the past week, and we'd come up with a dozen really solid ideas. Eduardo had advised us to go home and think long and hard before making our final decision. The morning after my run-in with the thug in the alley, me and the other Nimrods gathered in Norman's garage to eat donuts and finally reveal our costume choices.

Norman went first. He stood up and licked his fingers clean of donut glaze. "So, I was thinking about going as Pirate Ninja," he said.

I felt my brain start to short circuit.

"Say what?" I said.

"The way I figured it, Pirate Ninja's almost better than the comic book heroes. He's like Kings Cove's *own* superhero. My mom was the one who mentioned it, and since she normally suggests I go as either a hobo or an inflatable balloon, I actually thought this was a pretty good idea."

"Yes," agreed Quentin. "Pirate Ninja is pretty cool."

"Wait," I said, looking around at all of my friends. "You're all serious? You actually think Pirate Ninja is a legit superhero?"

Eduardo gave me a funny look, and Freddy swallowed another booger. "You don't?" they both asked.

I shrugged. "I mean, you guys act like he's a real superhero. He's just a..." I stopped.

"A what?" pressed Eduardo. "He's just a what?"

"I have no idea what he is. Some weirdo, probably. That's what the police keep saying." I couldn't risk the guys thinking I was a big Pirate Ninja fan.

"Yeah, Archie, but you should know better than anyone," said Eduardo.

I felt myself starting to sweat. Uh-oh. What did Eduardo know?

"Why should *I* know better than anyone?"

Eduardo rolled his eyes. "Because, stupid: you're an even bigger comic book nerd than me. You know the police never trust the new superhero. Especially at first."

I relaxed. "I guess you're right. Maybe Pirate Ninja will turn out to be okay. But Norm, you're not really going as him for Halloween, are you?"

Norman grinned and lifted a finger. "I said I was *thinking* about it. But no, I had a better costume in the works. My mom and I have been working on it for a while. I wasn't sure if it was going to work, but I think we figured it out. Want to see it?"

Uh, yeah, we wanted to see it.

Norm went inside, and when he came back down to the garage a few minutes later, he was wearing a Thing costume. You know, the Thing: Russ Grimm from the Fantastic Four. And this costume didn't just work. It was *incredible.* Not one of those pre-made off-the-rack jobs with lines painted to look like orange rocks. Nope, Norman had made papier-mâché rocks, and then his mom had hand-stitched them together into a costume that could only be called epic.

Next was Quentin's turn. He led off by giving us some boring statistics about how many girls had dressed up like Anna and Elsa from *Frozen* in recent years, how the number of Chewbacca costumes wasn't near what you might expect, and how small kids often don't wear the costumes of large superheroes. Finally he got on with it, pulled a Thor costume out of his backpack, and slipped it on. I had figured with Norman going as Thing, Quentin might want to go as Reed Richards, Mr. Fantastic. But when I asked him about that, he said he was set on Thor—for no other reason than that he carries a hammer. Quentin *really* wanted to carry a hammer.

Freddy said that he, too, had thought about going as Pirate Ninja, since they had become so close in their last adventure together. But for Freddy, there really was no choice to be made. He was, of course, planning to come as Galactic Booger Boy! Since none of us wanted to see or even think about what that costume looked like, we ignored him completely.

And last was Eduardo. I had been afraid that he might come as all six letters in the word "Nimrod." Then I thought it was possible he might come as Green Lantern, because sometimes Eduardo liked to champion underdogs, and the Green Lantern is a pretty darn weak superhero.

He disappeared to the back of the house to put on his costume, then came back to Norman's garage for the big reveal.

I was both right and wrong.

Right in that Eduardo did indeed choose a superhero underdog. Wrong in that I didn't understand just how far he was willing to go in choosing an underdog.

When I saw the iconic yellow cape, red shirt, and green gloves and tights, I thought I was hallucinating. But when Eduardo put both hands on his hips and puffed his chest out, it was clear that I was not.

"Robin?" I asked.

"You came as the Boy Wonder?" asked Quentin.

There was a long, uncomfortable moment of silence. Then Norman, Quentin, Freddy and I burst out laughing.

"That's enough," Eduardo said. "Laugh all you want. But you know how McGinley and that idiot Barry call us Nimrods, but they don't realize that Nimrod was an awesome warrior from the Bible?"

"You're telling me that Robin is secretly the greatest superhero of all time?" I said.

Eduardo pulled out a piece of paper. "Telling you? No, I'm going to *prove* it to you."

CHAPTER 3

Eduardo's epic attempt at defending the Boy Wonder lasted the entire walk to school, every time our teacher turned toward the board during class, and all through lunch. Even at recess, hanging out at the light pole with the Nimrods, Eduardo was *still* making his case for Robin's coolness. Though by this point, everyone was pretty well ignoring Eduardo. Freddy was being Freddy, Norman was practicing his raspy Russ Grimm voice, and

Quentin was busy on his tablet, developing a trick-or-treating route that would get us the maximum amount of candy with a minimum amount of effort.

And that's when something really unexpected happened: somebody else showed up.

Freddy noticed it first. His mouth fell open, and he even stopped picking his nose. Quentin jumped into the air and landed in Norman's lap. Thankfully, Eduardo and I played it much cooler. He ran one way, and I ran right into him, and we both fell to the ground.

Because, you see, this wasn't just *somebody*.

This was a girl.

And not just *any* girl.

"Eduardo," I said. "Is that the tallest girl in the world?"

"No," he said. "She just seems huge because we're still lying on the ground."

I immediately stood up. He was right. She wasn't sixteen feet tall like I'd first thought. This girl was about my size. She had long blonde hair. Glasses. She was holding a yellow piece of paper.

"So, you guys are taking clients?" she asked.

Eduardo and I exchanged confused looks.

"Um, are you talking to us?" I said.

She waved the flyer. "It says right here, to meet at the light pole. You *are* the Nimrods, aren't you?"

Eduardo snapped out of it first. "Of course

we're the Nimrods. But what are you talking about?" He ripped the paper out of the girl's hands. It read:

The Mighty Nimrods
led by
The Galactic Booger Boy

Now taking Clients!
If you need it found, solved, or fought,
The Nimrods can get it done.

Mighty Nimrods
P.O. Box, The LightPole

"So, which one of you is the Galactic Booger Boy?" The girl turned toward me. "It's you, isn't it?"

I wanted to be extremely offended that she thought I could be the Galactic Booger Boy, but before I could say anything, I had been knocked out of the way by Freddy. He stood in front of the girl with an enormous gooey booger in one hand.

"Galactic Booger Boy at your service."

The girl immediately turned around. I think she might have been throwing up. "I change my mind. I really don't want to meet Galactic Booger Boy. Can you make him go away?"

"Freddy," said Eduardo. "I need a ten-minute booger timeout."

Freddy made a face. "How about one minute?"

"Five minutes."

"Fine."

"Um," Eduardo said to the girl. "You can turn around now."

The girl slowly turned around. When she saw that Freddy had his hands behind his back and wasn't about to do anything, she relaxed.

Eduardo pointed to the flyer. "Can someone explain to me what is going on?"

"I just wanted to know if you guys are really taking clients," said the girl.

"Yes, we are," said Freddy. "I made the flyer."

"Why?" Eduardo asked.

"It's pretty straightforward," Freddy said. "When I was in that helicopter with Pirate Ninja—oh, have I mentioned that Pirate Ninja and I were in the same helicopter together?"

We all groaned.

"Only about a thousand times," said Eduardo.

"So there we were," Freddy continued, "fighting the forces of evil together—when something almost magical happened."

My ears perked up. "Something magical?"

Freddy shrugged. "Or cosmic. I'm not sure of the right word, but something happened... and I'm pretty sure I sucked up some of Pirate Ninja's special powers."

I coughed, and Eduardo laughed. "Powers? You have special powers now?"

Freddy shrugged. "Pretty sure." He took his hands out from behind his back and held them out in front of him. "Yep. No doubt about it. The Galactic Booger Boy has got something pretty special running through him now."

When he started to move his fingers toward his nose, Eduardo yelled, "No, Freddy, STOP!"

Freddy stopped his fingers only inches from his nose, then put them back behind his back.

"So," Freddy said, "I figured with my newfound superhero powers, and the fact that Pirate Ninja and I worked so well together in— well, you know the thing that rhymes with gelicopter—I thought it was time we start helping Pirate Ninja out."

"Helping him out?" I said.

"Yeah. So I made those flyers, put them up around school... so if anybody needs some bad guys found, some crimes solved, we Nimrods will handle it. You know, take a little bit off of Pirate Ninja's plate."

The girl waved the flyer. "I saw it this morning, figured it wouldn't hurt to try. But if you guys aren't really taking cases..." She began to turn around.

"Stop," I said.

I looked at Eduardo, who seemed annoyed, as usual. I said to him, "I mean, we could try, couldn't we?"

He went bug-eyed. "Are you suggesting we talk to a girl? On purpose? This is highly unusual."

"How bad can it be really be?" I said. "Plus, maybe she actually likes Robin."

Eduardo shot me an evil look. "Fine. We'll listen to what she has to say."

"Really?" the girl said. "Great. Well, I'm Katie."

None of us said anything.

"Katie Simpson. You're Eduardo, right?"

Eduardo looked my way. His lips were trembling. It was like he didn't know what to do next.

"I think I've been in your class like my whole life," said Katie. "But I don't think we've ever talked before."

"You can do this," I whispered to Eduardo.

He nodded, took a deep breath, then turned

back to Katie. "That is true. We have never talked before."

"Why is that?" Katie asked.

"Because we are boys," said Eduardo.

"And what does that have to do with anything?"

"Well, um, for one, boys are awkward."

"Super awkward," I said.

"And for another, boys are like, super scared of girls," Eduardo said.

I gave him a reassuring pat on the back. "You're doing great," I whispered.

Katie frowned. "That's silly. Why are you scared of girls?"

Eduardo's face changed, and I could tell the light had come on. He was ready to argue. Eduardo was back. "Because girls are scary," he said. "It would be much easier if we didn't have to talk to girls until we were all old, like in our sixties, like my parents."

"Eduardo," said Freddy. "You're parents aren't sixty. They're in their thirties."

Eduardo shrugged. "Sixties, thirties, it's all the same. It's all old. Anyways, it doesn't matter. I'm violating my *Don't talk to girls* rule because you said you had a case. The struggle of good versus evil is more important than my no girl rule. So, Ms. Simpson, you've got my attention. But I warn you: this better be important."

Katie shook her head. "Boys are super weird."

"Yes," said Eduardo. "I almost forgot that one. We are awkward, scared, and super weird. But Halloween is coming up, and we don't want anything to distract us from that. So this better be important. What's your case?"

She spread her hands wide. "*The Case of the Missing Candy,*" she said dramatically.

Missing candy? I didn't know about the other guys, but this girl had *my* attention.

"Say no more," said Eduardo. "We'll take your case."

"But I haven't even told you about it," Katie said.

"But I know it's important," Eduardo said, "because nothing, and I mean *nothing*, is more important than candy."

CHAPTER 4

"It first happened two years ago," Katie said. "It was the first year my friends and I really made a big candy score. Our bags were super full."

"We talking plastic pumpkins here?" Eduardo asked.

Katie sneered. "Plastic pumpkins? What do you think we are, amateurs? No, I'm talking pillowcases. Big pillowcases. And they were full. So, we were just heading back to my house to sort our candy—when six ninjas jumped out of the bushes."

"Ninjas?" I said.

Katie nodded. "They stole our candy bags, jumped over the bushes, and ran away. And you know the really sick thing? They were laughing. And me?" She jabbed a thumb into her chest. "I've never cried so much in my life."

Eduardo held his hand up and narrowed his eyes. "Wait a second. Wait just a second. Why were you crying so much?"

"Because they took my candy."

"And you like candy?"

"What are you talking about? I luuurrrve candy."

Eduardo leaned over. "Did she just say luuurrrve?"

"It means really, 'really really love' in girl talk."

Eduardo nodded, then turned back to Katie. "But you're a girl," he said. "I thought girls liked stuff like carrot sticks, and bottled water, and salads."

Katie snatched the flyer out of Eduardo's hands. "If you think that, then you really *are* a Nimrod."

Eduardo smiled. "So you think I'm a mighty warrior?"

"Arggghhh!" said Katie. "Why did I even bother?"

"Eduardo," I whispered. "Not cool, man."

Eduardo shook his head. "Fine. I'm sorry. Listen, don't go. I just thought candy was a boy thing. I honestly didn't know girls loved candy or sorting candy or anything else about Halloween."

"Well, we do. We like candy just as much as boys. And can you imagine how you would have felt if someone stole your candy?"

"Honestly, and with no exaggeration," said Norman unexpectedly, "I can't think of anything worse in the entire world."

"How about if an asteroid the size of Texas hit our planet?" Quentin asked.

"Hard to say," said Norman, "but I'm leaning towards the stolen candy being worse."

"So you want us to solve a two-year-old candy

caper?" Eduardo asked Katie.

"I didn't finish. Last year, same thing. The girls and I made another killer candy haul and decided to take a different route—but boom: this time six pirates jump out from behind a fence, take our candy, and run away."

"Wait a second," I said. "First a group of ninjas steals your candy, and then a group of pirates steals your candy?"

Katie nodded. "And that brings us to this year. The girls and I are tired of these candy culprits. We don't want it to happen again this year."

A silence fell upon all of us. Norman looked sad. Quentin was looking up from his computer. Freddy wasn't even trying to sneak in a booger.

I think we all understood the seriousness of the situation.

"Katie," I said, "we'll take your case. Right, Eduardo?"

"Right, Archie. We will. Of course we will. The world can't allow candy culprits to roam the world freely, stealing any candy they desire. As long as I'm a Nimrod, I'll do what I can to stop such madmen."

"You actually kind of sounded like a superhero there," Katie said.

Eduardo beamed. "I did? I mean, of course I did, miss."

"Miss," she said. Then she giggled. "I wrote as much as we could remember on the back of your flyer, but if you have any more questions... you can just ask us tonight."

"Tonight?" I said. "Don't you mean tomorrow at school?"

"No," she said. "Tonight. You're going, right?"

"Going where?"

She grabbed something out of her back pocket. It was another flyer. A pink flyer. "I saw your Nimrod flyer when I was handing out flyers for the dance."

"D-d-dance?" Eduardo said. He grabbed her flyer and all us boys gathered around, staring at it.

"Yeah. Tonight's the Halloween Dance. It's the first year we've had one. Us girls have been begging the school to do it for years. You wear your costumes, drink punch, and dance. It'll be fun."

"But we can't go to a dance," I said.

Katie folded her arms. "Why?"

"Because we're boys."

"Oh, and you're awkward, and scared of girls, and super weird?"

"Yes!" I said.

"Too bad," Katie said. "I was hoping you would go just for the candy."

"Candy?" all four of us boys said in unison.

She smiled, then pointed to the bottom of the flyer. "It says it right there. Each boy who comes to the dance gets one free bag of candy."

We were stunned. Speechless. Helpless. And Katie knew it. She just kept grinning. And when she knew she had us, she said: "I'll see you tonight, boys."

And then she turned and walked away.

And we knew what we had to do.

"Boys," said Eduardo. "Looks like we're going to our first dance. Now saddle up, Nimrods. Let's ride."

And the four of us galloped back to class.

CHAPTER
5

It didn't take very long for the reality to set in.

We'd agreed to go to a Halloween Dance.

With girls.

A *dance.*

With *girls.*

Girls.

What we'd agreed to in a moment of candy-inspired euphoria had now become a cold, hard reality.

We had to go to a dance.

Let that sink in.

The boys and I had the entire afternoon to let it sink in. And that didn't help. Not at all.

So what did we end up doing?

Come on! They were offering free bags of candy. We couldn't have turned that down even if we'd wanted to. It's part of the boy code. When offered candy, thou shalt take it every single time.

And so, it was with quite a bit of fear and trembling that we Nimrods approached the Kingman Middle School gym that evening.

Norman was dressed as Thing. Quentin was the smallest Thor I'd even seen, and Eduardo was the Boy Wonder.

And me? I never did tell you what I decided on. Drumroll, please...

I went as... Hawkeye!

You know, Clint Barton? Hawkeye. Member of the Avengers. Underwhelming, you say? I'm no better than Eduardo? Well, unlike Eduardo, at least I didn't try to argue that Hawkeye was the greatest superhero in the world. I just thought he was cool. Plus, he's got a bow. All Robin has is sharp language. I had a bow that shot twelve different kinds of arrows. Enough said.

Anyway, back to that little dance thing.

Having never been to a Halloween dance—or any kind of a dance for that matter—I had no idea what to expect. But the creepy music and giant spider webs outside the school gym were a good start. We Nimrods walked through a long creepy tunnel, which then opened up into the lobby of the gymnasium.

Where girls were handing out bags of candy.

"Oh boy," said Norman in his raspy Russ Grimm voice.

"Wow," Eduardo said. "I wasn't going to believe it until I saw it. But it's true. It's really true."

We grabbed our bags of candy and walked

through the long lobby toward the gymnasium. I didn't know what awaited us inside, but with a bag full of candy in my hands, I didn't much care.

And then, before we could enter, the English teacher, Ms. Snowbanks, stopped us. "No candy in the dance."

"What?" Eduardo said.

"We don't need you animals any more hopped up on sugar than you already are." She pointed to a room filled with other bags of candy. "Put it in there with the rest. It'll be locked up until the end of the night."

She grabbed the bags from us and threw them in the room. Then she pushed us all into the gymnasium.

And that was that.

"We've been tricked!" Eduardo said.

"Bamboozled!" I added.

"Hoodwinked!" cried Norman.

"Boogerwiped!" yelled Freddy.

"That's not actually a thing," I said.

"It actually *is* a thing," said Freddy. "Here, I'll show you."

I quickly turned away from Freddy and began to look around. The entire gymnasium was decorated. But not with spiders and webs and scary things. Not even superheroes. No, there was a lot of... pink. Quite a bit of purple, too. And ponies, unicorns, and witches. But not scary witches. These were cute witches. Some were riding even cuter ponies.

It was exactly how a five-year-old girl's birthday cake would be decorated. This did *not* look like Halloween.

"Nimrods," Eduardo said. "Huddle up. Listen, we have been tricked by some serious eighth-degree black belt tricksters here. I say we saddle up, gallop out of here, and never come back."

"You mean until tomorrow when we have gym class?" Freddy said.

"Right, we never come back until tomorrow

the period right before lunch."

Norman folded his arms. "No."

"No, what?" Eduardo asked.

"I'm not leaving. Not without my candy."

"But Norman, that means we'll have to stay here for the whole dance. In the land of ponies and fairy tales," I said.

"Sometimes a Thing's got to do what a Thing's got to do," said Norman.

Eduardo leaned over to me and whispered, "I haven't seen Norman this determined about something since the day they released the new outrageous-sized Blizzard at Dairy Queen. It might not be good to mess with him."

And so it was settled. We would stay.

We wouldn't *enjoy* it... but we would stay.

Now, never having been to a dance before, I didn't exactly know the rules. But within minutes of looking around, I was pretty sure I had figured them out. All the boys stood on one side of the gym, and all the girls stood on the other. A DJ was getting ready on the stage, and several teachers stood around here and there, while a very lonely crystal ball hung from the middle of the gym ceiling.

The Nimrods and I joined the other boys, who, not surprisingly, were separated into ninjas and pirates. We Nimrods were the only ones dressed differently. And when the music started—and the girls started to make their way onto the dance floor—that became a big problem.

Because, you see, the girls didn't go anywhere near the pirates and ninjas. Instead, they came right for us.

"Uh-oh," I said. They moved toward us like members of the zombie apocalypse. The one in front was dressed like a Disney princess. I recognized her at once.

It was Katie Simpson.

"Hey, Archie, right? Well, considering this is a dance and all, I was wondering if maybe, quite possibly, you know... you might like to dance?"

There it was. The word rattled around in my brain like a pinball.

My palms got sweaty. Okay, let's be real. *Everything* got sweaty.

I swallowed hard. "Um, d-d-dance?"

"Yes, Archie. Dance. That's where we are, a dance. And as you can see, nobody is dancing. So, I was thinking, maybe it takes a Disney princess and Robin Hood to get this party started?"

I gasped. "Robin Hood? You think I'm dressed like Robin Hood?"

Katie laughed. "Relax, Clint, I knew it was you."

"Wait—you know about Clint Barton?"

"Born in Iowa, parents killed in a car accident, raised in the circus, goes on to become Hawkeye, a member of the Avengers? Yeah, I know about Clint Barton."

I felt my mouth fall open.

Then I looked at Norman, Eduardo, Freddy, and Quentin to see if they had any advice. All their mouths were hanging open too.

It was weird. I'd been leaving my house most nights to battle the bad guys of Kings Cove, California—yet somehow that didn't seem so scary anymore. Not compared to this. Dancing? With a *girl*? In front of *other people*?

This was absolutely terrifying.

But for some reason, it was thinking about Pirate Ninja that helped me out. Or rather, thinking about my superhero coach, Grievous. The way I figured it, if he ever got wind that I was too scared to dance with a girl, he would probably make me train so hard that I would regret it to my dying day.

And this girl knew who Hawkeye was... so maybe she wasn't the worst girl in the world to dance with.

I took a deep breath. "I guess the answer is—"

Someone let out a bloodcurdling scream.

Katie and I both jumped. We turned toward the gym lobby, where Ms. Snowbanks was screaming.

"Help! Help!" she yelled.

We rushed over to her. "Ms. Snowbanks, what happened?"

"It's gone, it's all gone."

"What's gone?" I said.

But all she could do was point. I followed her finger to a room with an open door.

I heard a single scream first, but it was soon

joined by an entire chorus of screams. Ahead of me, ninjas and pirates started jumping up and down and freaking out.

I thought somebody had died.

But I soon found out it was worse.

Much worse.

The room behind Ms. Snowbanks where all the candy had been stored?

It was empty.

Completely empty.

A perfectly round hole had been cut into the sheet metal that formed the exterior wall of the gym.

The kids of Kingman School had been robbed.

Of their *candy*.

If you have never witnessed a gym full of middle school kids who've just found out their candy's been stolen, then I can't possibly describe the scene.

But it was carnage. Pure carnage. Imagine the world after that giant Texas-sized asteroid collides with it. What I was witnessing was twice as bad.

And Norman? He was struggling more than anyone. At first he was howling like an injured animal. Then the sadness turned to rage.

"I'm gonna get him," he said.

"Who are you going to get?" Eduardo asked.

"Whoever took this candy, that's who," he said.

That, of course, was the question: who on earth could have, and would have, pulled off such a crime?

Mr. Ned Pepper, our school's head of security, came running into the gym.

"I've seen the security video," he said breathlessly. "I've just seen the video. It was him. He did it."

"Who did it?" Norman asked.

Ned Pepper cleared his throat. "I'm sorry to say, but... it was Pirate Ninja."

CHAPTER
6

I was more shocked than anyone to learn that
Pirate Ninja was the one responsible for the
sensational candy caper.

Considering that I *was* Pirate Ninja.

But there was the school's head of security,
Mr. Pepper, with his bald head and handlebar
mustache, claiming it was so. And now he was
holding up a small piece of paper that he said
confirmed what he had witnessed on the
security video.

"It appears," he said, "that this is the note confessing to the crime. We found it on the school lawn. He even signed it. Right here. PIRATE NINJA. Even spelled it right."

That was an odd thing to say. Did Ned Pepper come from a world where people usually did *not* spell their names correctly?

Anyways, the news set everybody off. Eduardo and Quentin got involved in a heated discussion about what this crime did to Pirate Ninja's superhero ranking. Eduardo thought this made Pirate Ninja seem more dangerous, which might help make him even scarier to the bad guys. Quentin wasn't buying it.

We went back in the gym, where I found Freddy sucking down fruit punch and doing that other thing he's usually doing, and Norman sitting cross-legged on the floor moaning in pain.

"It's not like somebody died," I said to him, trying to cheer the big fella up.

"I know," he slobbered. "It's worse than that. Much worse."

"I just can't believe Pirate Ninja would do something like this," Eduardo said.

I couldn't either. Something bad was going on, and I needed to be careful. I knew that I, Pirate Ninja, definitely did *not* cut a hole through that wall. I did *not* steal a half ton of candy. And I *certainly* didn't leave a note confessing to the crime.

"What if it wasn't him?" I asked.

Eduardo stopped scratching his chin. "So yesterday you thought Pirate Ninja was a weirdo, and today you're taking his side?"

"Just hear me out. I mean, if you stole something, would you leave a note confessing to the crime?" I asked.

"Are you speaking of me, Eduardo, or me, Robin, Boy Wonder, world's greatest superhero?"

"How long are you going to keep at it with the Robin's-a-great-superhero thing?" I asked.

"As long as it takes."

"No," Quentin said. "Nobody would leave a note confessing to the crime. Unless..."

"Unless what?" Eduardo asked.

"Unless someone is trying to frame Pirate Ninja," I said.

Quentin nodded. "Remember how mad District

Attorney Vincent was at his last press conference? He said he was convinced Pirate Ninja was the one really responsible for the prank. If I had to guess, he's trying to set Pirate Ninja up again."

Eduardo shook his head. "I don't get it. Vincent also said he was going to make it his mission to find out who Pirate Ninja really was. How does this help him?"

Quentin's eyes lit up behind his glasses. "Don't you see? This is the next best thing. Vincent doesn't have any idea who Pirate Ninja is... so he's decided to make Pirate Ninja look bad. If he makes everybody in Kings Cove hate Pirate Ninja, then Pirate Ninja won't be able to operate, won't be able to help people. And best of all for Vincent, he won't be able to mess up the Vulture's crime organization."

I looked at Norman, who was still sniffling about his lost bag of treats. "And is there any better way to get people to hate you than to steal a bunch of kids' candy?"

"Wait a second." The voice came from behind me. I turned around to find myself face to face with Katie Simpson.

"I couldn't help but hear you boys talking," she said. "You don't think Pirate Ninja did it either, do you?"

"*You* don't think it was Pirate Ninja?"

She shook her head. "Heck no. Remember my case? The one you Nimrods are supposed to solve for me?"

"I sort of forgot about that!"

"Yeah, well, I didn't. This wasn't the first incident of large-scale candy theft in this town. Like I said, it happened two years ago, and it happened again last year."

"*And* it happened again tonight," Eduardo said.

"Exactly," said Katie. "You want to know my theory? You find out who stole my candy... and you'll figure out who was really wearing that Pirate Ninja costume tonight. You figure that out, and you'll get your candy back."

"Hard to argue with logic like that," I said.

"Archie," said Eduardo, "I have to agree. Saddle up, Nimrods. It's time to ride."

And together we galloped out of the gym.

CHAPTER 7

The next day, my worst fears were revealed in the headline on the front page of the newspaper:

PIRATE NINJA STRIKES AGAIN!

It was followed by a big photo of the hole in the wall of the Kingman Middle School gym. Under that were two more photos: one of the empty room, and another of Norman sobbing.

The reporter had talked to the police, and the detective in charge of the investigation had said that "the ongoing activity of the Pirate Ninja paints a complicated portrait. In addition to fighting crime, he is also himself a criminal." He told the reporter that they "might be dealing with a Jekyll and Hyde type character" and finding the Pirate Ninja was of the "utmost importance."

And then came the real clincher. The mayor and the police chief were calling on all the great citizens of Kings Cove. After trick-or-treating was completed, the rest of Halloween would be a community-wide "Find Pirate Ninja Night."

I put the paper down.

"You've got to be kidding me."

I felt heavy breathing behind me and spun around. McGinley was there, running his hand through his head of black, moppy hair.

He was pointing at the newspaper.

"We're gonna find that Pirate Ninja punk tonight, Archie from Omaha."

"Good for you," I said.

He shrugged. "The police are bringing us in as

consultants, since we fought that weirdo once and lived to tell about it."

"He doesn't kill people, McGinley. Everybody's lived to tell about it."

"Yeah, Archie, but not everyone's a ninja. Am I right?"

He winked at me then walked off, his ninjas following behind like little ducklings. Very stupid, annoying, ninja ducklings, following possibly the dumbest boy I'd ever met in my life.

So the whole town really *was* going to be looking for Pirate Ninja tonight. Which was a serious problem.

I took the blue note out of my pocket and read it once again:

October 31. Downtown. The Mother of All Jobs. The Vulture.

This was downright crazy. Something bad was going down, and whether they knew it or not, Kings Cove *needed* Pirate Ninja. But Pirate Ninja wouldn't be able to get half a mile from downtown without being spotted.

It looked like I had a busy Halloween night ahead of me. Somehow I had to go trick-or-treating with my friends, help the Nimrods figure out who'd been stealing Katie Simpson and her friends' candy, make sure that whoever was doing it was also the same person who stole the candy from the Halloween dance, and, last but not least, stop the Vulture and his crime organization from pulling off the Mother of All Jobs downtown—on the very night the mayor had declared "Find Pirate Ninja Night."

I was crazy to even consider stopping the Vulture. I knew that much.

But I also knew this: there was nobody else to stop him. And in a world in which the Vulture was trying to make everybody on earth believe that Pirate Ninja was bad, I had no choice but to show that Pirate Ninja was truly a hero.

And how was I going to do all of this?

I had no earthly idea.

But the first step was the light pole.

Quentin was busy at work on his tablet computer. Norman had a stick and was drawing something in the dirt. In a refreshing change, Freddy was not picking his nose. Instead, he was doing all sorts of crazy somersaults in the grass. Eduardo was laughing at him.

"What's Freddy doing?" I asked.

"Well," Eduardo said quietly, "Freddy received an email from the National Academy of

Superheroes saying that they were coming by the school tomorrow to give him a tryout."

"Say what?"

"Yeah, I emailed him from a fake email account. I thought it would be funny. I included a list of fake superhero exercises he could do."

Freddywas on his hand and knees now. He appeared to be smooshing his face into the dirt.

"What is he doing?"

"Ahh," said Eduardo. "That's the exercise where you push a pebble across the dirt with nothing but your nose. It's supposed to work the olfactory glands. For superhero sense of smell and all."

"Eduardo, that's genius."

He shrugged. "Hey, even I get tired of all the booger-picking sometimes."

"Guys," said Quentin. "I think I've narrowed down our search area."

"Our search area?" I asked.

Quentin looked up. "I took the data Katie gave

us about where the candy was stolen the two previous years, and I mapped those locations."

He showed us a Google map of Kings Cove with two green stars on it.

"I also put in the data of what house Katie said they were heading back to each night. The first year they were heading back to Katie's house, and the second year they were heading back to Angela Treinen's house."

"And who is Angela Treinen again?" Eduardo asked.

Quentin wrinkled his nose. "She's been in your class the last four years, you sometimes carpool together, and she's been your science lab partner for the last three months."

Eduardo held up his hands. "I had no idea."

"So anyway, then I took the GPS coordinates of each location, ran them through a program, and bam, I got this."

Quentin showed us a red circle that covered an area of about three neighborhood blocks.

"This is the area it's most likely the candy thieves are coming from?" I asked.

"That's right," said Quentin.

"What about the candy theft at the gym? Why isn't that one of the data points?" Eduardo asked.

Quentin pushed his glasses up his nose. "I don't think it's the same people. Katie said it was a group of six ninjas, then six pirates. And then all of a sudden, to pull off a much more dangerous mission, only one person does it? No. I don't see it. I think that third crime is unrelated to the first two."

"But Katie was sure that if we figured out who stole her candy, we would figure out who stole the candy from the gym," I said.

"Sorry, Archie," said Eduardo. "Best we can do is lie to Norman at this point. But hey, if we help Katie and her friends catch their candy culprits, then they'll give us a cut of their candy haul. That might be the best we can do this year."

"Okay, so how exactly do we do this? How do we catch these Halloween hooligans?"

"It all starts with these." Quentin unzipped his backpack and handed me something small and black.

"Walkie-talkies?" I said.

"Don't worry," he said. "I've got a plan."

After he explained it, I had only one question.

"And you guys are absolutely certain that I am the one who has to do it?"

"Yep," said Eduardo. "The Galactic Booger Boy can't be trusted—for obvious reasons— Norman's too fragile right now, and Quentin and I are absolutely scared to death of girls. No, Archie, you are the only one who can do it."

"Fine," I said. "I'll do it. But how are we going to figure out who's behind the Halloween Party theft?"

Quentin pulled a small briefcase out of his bag. "By conducting a little crime scene investigation of our own."

"But we can't get near that place. Ms. Snowbanks and Mr. Pepper have kept that area under supervision all day."

Eduardo smiled and nodded his chin at Norman. "Thankfully, Norman's been working on a diversion."

CHAPTER 8

The first thing we needed was access to the crime scene. You see, ever since the dance, Ms. Snowbanks had been standing vigil at the scene of the crime—or, as she was now calling it, her *great embarrassment*. We needed to get Snowbanks away from there for a few minutes. And that's where Freddy and Norman came in.

Thankfully, Norman's mom had been very concerned about her son since he lost all his candy. She had told him she'd be on sugar alert all day in case he needed something. And Norman most certainly needed something. Specifically, a pie. Preferably the cream variety.

The diversion plan was fairly simple. Freddy would take a large, slimy booger and chase Norman with it. And all the while, Norman would be carrying a large chocolate cream pie. Why? Because he's Norman. We thought that was a good enough reason.

When Eduardo, Quentin, and I had moved into position, Freddy and Norman went to work from their position at the far end of the school commons. Freddy yelled, "I'm gonna booger wipe you if it's the last thing I do!" Norman screamed as he ran.

Predictably, Ms. Snowbanks moved a bit to see the commotion. But she didn't move far enough to leave her post.

That was about to change.

Freddy kept yelling and chasing, Norman kept running, and that pie shook as much as

Norman's belly. And they were both coming right for Ms. Snowbanks.

I could tell she knew what was happening when her whole body tensed and she threw her hands up in the air. But by then, it was too late. The collision made a terrible noise, and Snowbanks, Norman, and Freddy all screamed.

But Norman and that chocolate cream pie both did their job. Ms. Snowbanks was completely covered in chocolate pie filling—not to mention one very gnarly green booger that had made its way to the side of her cheek.

When Freddy pointed that out, she screamed, sprinted across the commons to the parking lot, and jumped into the creek on the other side. And that meant we had the crime scene all to ourselves.

While Norman started licking the chocolate pie off the grass, Quentin opened up his crime scene kit and put the rest of us to work.

Eduardo did a physical examination of the room, while I took photographs. Quentin dusted for prints. I was taking pictures of the hole in the wall when Eduardo raised his hand.

"I might have something here."

Quentin came over to see what Eduardo had found. He pulled some tweezers from his kit, leaned in, and pulled out something small and blue. He held it up and squinted at it.

"Appears to be a torn piece of clothing."

Eduardo scratched his chin. "I've seen the illustrations the paper runs of this Pirate Ninja. I don't think I remember seeing any navy blue."

"Me neither," I said.

"If this came from the thief, the real thief, the one who's framing Pirate Ninja..." said Eduardo.

"... then this piece of cloth could help us find him," I said.

"I've got his fingerprint now, too," Quentin added.

Norman stopped licking the grass long enough to say, "Sorry to burst your bubble, guys, but how on earth can a fingerprint and a bit of cloth help us find the real thief?"

Quentin tapped his tablet. "I need to do some work."

We went over our plan at Quentin's garage that afternoon while he hacked into the fingerprint database at the police headquarters.

Thankfully, he had done this before, so it was a lot easier this time.

It took Quentin a half hour to check the fingerprints, but he got no matches from any of the criminals in the system.

"Try the students," I said. "Remember how Vincent took fingerprints and DNA samples from all the students when he was trying to figure out who did the prank?"

Quentin went to work. Fifteen minutes later, he looked up. "Nothing," he said.

"Then who could it be?" I asked.

"Remember, a person doesn't normally have their fingerprints in the system until they've committed a crime."

"So we're talking about someone who's never committed a crime?" Eduardo asked.

Quentin held up his finger. "Or maybe just someone who's never been caught."

CHAPTER 9

I had planned to wear my Hawkeye costume trick-or-treating, but now everything was different. I couldn't afford for my face to be seen. Not where I was going. The only other costume I had was my Pirate Ninja uniform, and I couldn't very well wear that. Especially not on "Find Pirate Ninja Night."

And so it was that I was forced to ask my mom for help.

She thought about it until her eyes lit up and

she almost exploded in giggles. "Wait. Just you wait!" She ran downstairs and came back a few minutes later with something very large.

And very purple.

That night my mother took several selfies of her in her witch's costume and me in my Barney the dinosaur costume.

Yep.

Barney.

Mom hugged me a lot, called me her baby, and generally embarrassed me beyond belief. Then I took the long and lonely walk into enemy territory.

You see, I was the Nimrod who would be meeting up with Katie and her friends and following them on their trick-or-treating journey.

Now you understand why I couldn't afford to be recognized. Hanging out with a group of girls on Halloween? Barney was embarrassing. But this was worse.

As per the plan, the rest of the Nimrods were doing a stakeout. Quentin was so certain the culprits came from his search area that he, Eduardo, Freddy, and Norman were strategically positioned in bushes and trees around the three-block area. The idea was simple. If the thieves stole the girls' candy yet again, I would follow them and communicate with the Nimrods. Their job was to find the culprits when they went back to their hideout.

Quentin was certain that the candy thieves would have a hideout.

And then?

Well, we hadn't really thought that part out. But somehow we were going to get the candy back.

And so I walked, or rather wobbled, toward Katie's neighborhood. The Barney head was so insanely hot that I kept it off for as long as I could.

I knew I was in trouble when I was still half a

block from Katie's home. I could hear the telltale sign of giggling.

Girl giggling.

I was a boy, completely alone, with no backup.

And I was heading into the belly of the beast.

Six twelve-year-old girls dressed up in princess outfits and makeup and all jazzed up on candy.

I really wished Grievous had given me some sort of training for this.

When the girls saw me, the giggling turned into squeals. I immediately threw on the Barney head, and by the time I got within spitting distance, Katie was working to settle them down.

"Hi, Katie," I said from inside my enormous purple head.

She leaned forward. "Archie? It's really you?"

"Unfortunately."

"What happened to Hawkeye?"

Could I tell her that I was too scared for the world to see me hanging out with girls on Halloween?

I could not.

"Long story," was all I could muster.

"Sorry about the girls," she said. "They just got a little excited when they saw you."

"But don't all of them go to school with me?"

"This is different. You know how all the boys at Kingman are super weird about pirates and ninjas?"

"Yeah."

"And then there's the Nimrods?"

"Yes."

"Well, the girls have concluded that you, Archie, might be the only normal boy in the entire school. So they're just kind of excited that you're here."

"The girls think I'm normal?" I said. My face started to feel like it was the same color as my costume.

Katie's face got weird too. "Listen, Archie, it's not, um, well... argghh." She shook her head.

Awkward.

My turn to talk. "So, um..."

Yeah. Awkward.

"I hear they've got no new leads on the thievery at the Halloween Dance," Katie said.

"How do you know that?" I asked.

"My dad is friends with Mr. Pepper, the security guy. Mr. Pepper is convinced the candy was stolen by Pirate Ninja, so he's not even investigating any further."

That was strange. It was his job to protect the school, after all. Now we were out on the mean streets of Kings Cove trying to solve this mystery? It's like we were doing his job for him.

"Well," I said, "I was thinking I would just stay behind you at a safe distance, follow you around, and see what happens."

She made eye contact, but only briefly. "Okay."

The girls took off, and I followed. All in all it was pretty uneventful. I learned that girls mostly approached Halloween like us boys. Oh, sure, there was a lot more giggling, and tons of hugging. What's with all the hugging?

But other than that? I was impressed by what I saw. These girls were serious about their candy. They knew which houses gave out the full-sized candy bars. Which houses gave out cans of pop. And which houses gave out healthy snacks like carrot sticks and raisins. Thankfully, they avoided those houses.

And because I was trick-or-treating alone, I had plenty of time to wonder about just who might be responsible for all the candy thievery.

The most obvious explanation was that it was either McGinley and the ninjas or Barry and the pirates. My own personal opinion was that it was the pirates—because stealing valuable cargo from people is kind of what pirates do. It also made sense that the first year they did it, they dressed up like ninjas so that people wouldn't know it was them. And then the following year, they went back to pirates in order to keep people confused.

But the more I thought about it, the more I didn't buy this explanation. Because truthfully, I didn't know if Barry was smart enough to speak in sentences of more than four words, let alone think of something like an actual plan.

And so I followed Katie Simpson and her friends around the whole night, always staying one house behind them, as me and my Barney costume did the most pathetic thing a twelve-year-old boy can do: solo trick-or-treating. Once in a while Katie would wave at me, and a couple times the entire group of girls broke out in a giggle fit as they turned and looked my way. The worst part of the night was when a huge group of preschoolers thought I was *really* Barney and they all limed up to give me a "Big Hug."

But finally, after two solid hours of candy collection, Katie and her group were ready to call it quits and head back to her house.

I clicked on my walkie-talkie and alerted the guys. "Eduardo, do you come in."

"Who is this Eduardo of whom you speak? I am the Boy Wonder, the single—"

"—greatest superhero in the world, yes, I get it," I said. "I still don't know why you're persisting in this madness, but if it shuts you up, then fine: Robin is the greatest superhero in the world. Satisfied?"

"I feel like you're not being sincere," Eduardo said through the crackle of the walkie-talkie.

"Eduardo! Of course I'm not being sincere. Argghhh... Listen, the girls are heading back to Katie's home. No sign of the candy culprits yet.

Will keep you apprised. Purple dinosaur, out!"

Katie and her friends were turning right at the corner up ahead. I lost sight of them as the overhanging branches of an oak tree seemed to swallow them up.

Then I felt it.

Something very creepy and very crawly had wrapped itself around my left leg. I looked down. It was definitely moving.

And it looked a lot like Buzz Lightyear.

"Big Hug," a four-year-old Buzz Lightyear said.

This Barney guy was kinda creepy.

"Can you sing your song?" the little boy asked.

By this time, three other kids had shown up. A five-year-old Elsa, a one-eyed pirate, and a ghost. "Can you, Barney? Can you please sing it?"

"Sing what?" I asked.

"You know," said Buzz. "I love you, you love me."

Oh, no! I'd almost forgotten about that song. And without waiting for me to start, the little kids sang it right in front of me, grinning like idiots. It reminded me of the time I was in kindergarten and mom took me to a showing of Barney live. Barney asked for volunteers, and somehow I got picked. I helped him sing that song in front of five thousand people. It was terrifying. In fact, even now, I could almost hear myself screaming.

Wait. I was hearing someone *else* scream. For real. This was no memory.

I turned. The screaming was coming from that behind that big oak tree.

The girls!

Me and my fat short purple legs ran as fast as they could. And when I turned the corner, Katie was shaking her fists and screaming at a van that was speeding away down the street, leaving a trail of charcoal gray exhaust fumes behind it.

All the girls were empty-handed.

"Was it them? The Halloween Hooligans?" I asked.

"You mean the Candy Culprits?" Katie said.

"Whatever."

"Yes, it was them. Six of them. Again."

"What'd they dress like this year?"

"Ghosts. Just bed sheets with holes for eyes. They jumped out of the bushes. Grabbed the candy. Then the van pulled up and they all got away."

"What color van?"

"Blue," she said. "It was an old van. Kinda beat up. I think it was blue. Hey, I thought you were going to help. Where were you?"

"Long story. Barney. 'I Love You.' You know?"

"You love me?"

"Oh, man—um—no—I didn't—" I quickly turned away and hit the button on the walkie-talkie. "Boy Wonder, Quentin, Nimrods. Full alert. The thieves just struck and hopefully are coming your way. I repeat. They are coming your way. Riding in an old, beat-up blue van. There are six of them, and they're dressed like ghosts. I repeat: dressed like ghosts."

I waited to hear their response... but there was nothing.

"Um, Archie?" Katie said, pointing at my walkie-talkie. "Doesn't it work better if you turn it on first?"

Idiot! Somehow I'd turned the whole walkie-talkie off. I flipped the switch, hit the button, then communicated my message again.

"Just saw a blue van," Quentin replied. "Norman, he's heading your way. I repeat, heading your way."

I took my Barney head off and handed it to Katie.

"Can you hold this, please?"

"No," she said. I think she must have gotten a whiff of how stinky it was.

I jumped out of the rest of the costume. "Then how about this part of him?"

She stepped away from it. "No again."

"Fine." As I started to run away, I shouted back, "Just leave it in the middle of the street—little kids will walk by and think that poor Barney got sliced in half. You'll have that on your conscience!"

"Where are you going?" Katie yelled.

"I'm going to get your candy back!"

Thanks to my Pirate Ninja training, it took me only ten minutes of running at top speed to reach the search area. Without the purple dinosaur suit, I felt like I was practically flying. As I ran, I heard two updates come from the walkie-talkie.

The first was Norman. He saw the van take a left and go up Perkins Street. He sounded really mad. Eduardo reminded him not to do anything stupid.

"Can I at least confront them, try to beat them up, and get the candy back?"

"No, Norman. That would be the very definition of something stupid. There are six of them. You have to do the opposite of that."

The second update came from all three of them. They were perched in a tree across the street from the driveway where the blue van had apparently pulled in.

"Archie, we saw all six ghosts exit the van and go into the large detached garage."

"You think this is McGinley or Barry?" I asked.

"Neither, Archie. Here's the thing: these kids are huge. In fact, if I had to guess, they're not kids. When was the last time you remember twelve-year-old boys driving around old vans?"

"Fair point," I said.

"Archie, these are adults."

"Adults are stealing candy from kids? From girls?" It was almost too much to imagine.

"And there's something else," Eduardo said.

"What?"

By now, I had reached the tree where the guys were perched. I stuck my foot into a crevice in the trunk, grabbed a branch, and hoisted myself up.

"Quentin found something," Eduardo said.

Quentin looked up from his tablet. "I hacked into the DMV and ran the license plate. I got a hit. It belongs to this address. But you won't believe who it belongs to."

"If you say Barney the dinosaur, I'm really going to freak out."

"Worse." Quentin held up the tablet for me to see.

I was staring at the bald head and handlebar mustache of the head of security at Kingman School.

Ned Pepper.

CHAPTER 10

"Mr. Pepper's one of the Halloween Hooligans?"

Eduardo nodded. "Appears so."

"But... does that mean he's the one who stole the candy from the gym?"

"Hmm," said Quentin. "I wonder." He started typing away, and in a few minutes, a smile formed on his face. "I never thought to check before, but apparently, they fingerprint the employees of the school—including Mr. Pepper. I just compared his fingerprints to the one I found on the edge of the hole in the gym, and guess what? It's a match. A perfect match."

"But Mr. Pepper said the video showed Pirate Ninja committing the crime," Freddy said.

Quentin twisted his mouth. Then he went back to banging away at his tablet. He seemed to be fighting with something on the screen. Quentin always got that way when he was up against a difficult problem. Finally, he took a breath and his face relaxed.

"Here it is," he said, turning his tablet for us all to see. It was video footage of the outside of the gym. It showed a man crouched low—a man who was definitely *not* dressed like Pirate Ninja. He cut a hole in the tin wall of the gym, then crawled inside. A couple minutes later, he came out with a huge bag and ran away.

The footage was grainy, but there was no doubt about it.

It was Ned Pepper.

Freddy held up a finger. "So even though Mr.

Pepper said he saw Pirate Ninja on the security video..."

"He's the only one who looked at the footage," Eduardo said. "And then he showed us the confession note. A note that *he* obviously wrote."

Quentin smiled. "And that navy blue piece of cloth we found at the scene of the crime? I bet that came from Mr. Pepper's security jacket!"

I heard a growl from Norman. And not from his stomach, as usual. This growl was coming from deep in the back of Norman's throat. He was slamming his fist into his hand, and I could have sworn I saw smoke coming out of his ears. "That no-good, stinkin', ratfink, double-crossing..." And then it got really bad. "Why would he do it? Why would he do this to a bunch of kids?"

"Guys," I said. "From the looks of it, it's not just Mr. Pepper. There's five other guys helping him. So the question is, why would *they* do this to a bunch of kids?"

Eduardo was scratching his chin. "This is all so confusing. But let's say Mr. Pepper is some sort of candy psycho and just can't help himself: he *has* to steal candy. Well if he is, then it makes sense for him to steal the candy at the Halloween Dance. I mean, it was a crime of opportunity. But stealing from a bunch of random girls from our school? That doesn't make sense at all."

"Unless..." Quentin said.

"Unless what?" I asked.

"Unless stealing from the girls is *also* a crime of opportunity."

"But none of those girls are Mr. Pepper's daughters," Eduardo said. "His kids are older. They've graduated high school, I think."

Then I remembered something Katie had said earlier in the evening.

"Katie told me earlier that Mr. Pepper still doesn't have any leads into who committed the crime. I asked her where she heard that. She said Mr. Pepper and her dad are good friends. *That* could be the connection—and that could be your opportunity."

"Katie's dad?" Quentin asked.

"Wait a second," said Eduardo. "You're suggesting that Katie's dad is part of this? Stealing candy from his own kid? That is seriously weird."

"Well, guys," I said. "I've come to learn that Kings Cove, California, is one seriously weird place. Almost all the boys are either into pirates or ninjas. The only normal kids are us Nimrods, and we hang out around a light pole, and one of our members never stops picking his boogers. The town's district attorney is actually the town's biggest thief, and a strange superhero helps to fight for freedom wherever there's trouble."

"You stole that last line from G.I. Joe, didn't you?" said Eduardo.

"Good catch, Eduardo. Listen, if Katie's dad is part of this, and we bust him, I'm not sure she'd ever be able to forgive him," I said. "I know I wouldn't."

"Okay," said Quentin. "So maybe there's a way to get the candy back without her having to find out her dad did it?"

"What do you have in mind?" Eduardo asked.

Seeing as this was Quentin, I was not surprised to learn he had a plan. And this one was simple.

We placed Norman behind the van in the driveway. If something bad happened, and the Halloween Hooligans ran out, we gave the Thing permission to release a candy conniption on those guys while we called 911.

But we hoped it wouldn't come to that.

We moved quietly across the street until we were just inches from Mr. Pepper's garage. I helped Quentin get on top of Eduardo's shoulders, and then we carefully moved him into position in front of the side window of the garage. Quentin pulled out his smartphone and started to record.

After two minutes, I pulled Quentin down, and we ran back across the street to our safe spot behind the tree.

"Well?" Norman said as he joined us.

"Jackpot," said Quentin. "Mr. Pepper and five other dads. Sitting around eating tons and tons of candy."

We sat in silence for a long moment. Grown men stealing candy from their kids? I mean, I loved candy as much as the next guy, but this was too much. And we needed to get that candy back!

On the school's website, Quentin was able to find Mr. Pepper's cell phone number. He was head of security, so it was listed as a number people could call in case of emergency.

We definitely had an emergency.

Quentin pulled out his phone. One more time, we all watched the video he'd taken: the video that showed Mr. Pepper and five other dads sitting in the garage, laughing, telling stories, and eating an insane amount of candy. Then Quentin attached the video to a text message he'd written to Mr. Pepper. This is what the message said:

Dear Halloween Hooligans! We know who you are. And so will your daughters.

And so will the school. And so will the police. And so will the world!!!! This video will be emailed to the police and loaded up on the school's website unless you comply with our demands. Load up all the candy into garbage bags. Place the garbage bags of candy onto the driveway. Then get into the blue van. And drive away. Any attempt to find us or to discover us... will result in this video being sent immediately. Sincerely, Your Worst Nightmare!

"I like it," growled Norman.

Quentin hit send.

Within seconds of sending the text, we heard a faint scream from the garage. Then we heard movement, shouting, and more movement. After a couple minutes, the big garage door opened up and six men came out, without their ghost costumes. Quentin filmed the entire thing.

They dropped big garbage bags onto the driveway, spent a few moments looking around, then got into the old blue van and drove away, leaving a charcoal gray exhaust trail in their wake.

Norman was normally the slowest of our group—but not on this night. He sprinted for those bags and gave them a truly "Big Hug."

We'd done it. We'd actually done it!

As each Nimrod stuffed a handful of candy into his mouth, I spotted one of those white ghost costumes in the garage. I picked it up and stuffed it into a candy bag. My night wasn't done yet.

The walk back to Katie Simpson's house was long and difficult, but it was glorious. As we Nimrods walked triumphantly past her front gate and up to her door, the door flew open, and Katie and five other girls screamed in excitement.

It was super embarrassing.

And a little awesome.

Katie looked at me and smiled. Then she looked at the other guys and shook her head. "Gotta hand it to you Nimrods: you did it. You really did it. So, who are the Halloween Hooligans after all? Is it McGinley?"

"Nope," said Freddy.

"So it's Barry and the pirates?"

"Nope," said Norman.

She pushed me with both hands. "Get out of here. Then who is it?"

I smiled sheepishly. "Can't say."

She gave me a crooked grin. "Can't? Or won't?"

"It's complicated. Let's just say it was the only way to get the candy. But we know who they are, we have the evidence, and if they ever, ever mess with you again, we'll let everyone know."

"You're really not gonna tell me?"

I shook my head.

"And how about the candy stolen from the gym?"

"Same hooligans. You were right about that."

"Of course I was right," Katie said. "Well, thanks, Archie. I owe you."

The guys and I took our cut of the missing candy. Katie and the girls said they would take the missing gym candy back to school the next day. I wasn't sure they trusted Norman to keep it safe.

We started to walk away, when Katie spoke behind us.

"So, are you guys helping out tonight with 'Find Pirate Ninja Night'?"

"I think we're too tired," I said. I was lying, of course.

She smiled. "Yeah, us too. See you around, Archie."

"See you around, Katie."

The Nimrods and I all agreed we'd been through enough already and didn't need the hassle of searching for Pirate Ninja. Plus, none of us wanted to find him. We hoped the Vulture *never* found him. And so we walked home, each of us stuffing our face full of candy.

When we got to the spot where we usually split up to go our separate ways, I went into the woods, as was my usual route. But instead of going home, I found my special bag under the flat rock by the tree I called the dirty oak. I took my Pirate Ninja uniform out of my bag and put it on. I slipped on my super boots and put on my eyepatch with the special super-vision lens. Then I made sure I had my wooden sword.

With an entire city looking for me, was I nuts to go out one more time?

Sure.

But the Vulture was pulling the mother of all jobs tonight.

And I couldn't let the people of Kings Cove down.

CHAPTER 11

Here's the thing. I might be crazy, but I wasn't stupid. I took that ghost costume out of my bag of candy, and I slipped it on over my Pirate Ninja uniform. I wasn't about to go running around Kings Cove in my Pirate Ninja uniform on "Find Pirate Ninja Night."

At least, not unless I had to.

I took my usual zigzag route downtown. It was a route that had become familiar to me over the last couple of months. When I arrived, I witnessed an incredible sight. Hundreds of Kings Cove residents, some still dressed in Halloween costumes, some not, were walking around the city, looking for Pirate Ninja.

So I pretended to be one of them.

But of course I wasn't looking for Pirate Ninja. I was looking for the bad guys. I and my super vision were most definitely looking for bad guys—and the mother of all jobs.

But after a couple hours of wandering the streets and alleys of downtown Kings Cove, I was getting tired... and I was beginning to think that maybe there really was no big job. Maybe it had all been called off when the "Find Pirate Ninja Night" had been declared.

But I figured I would check one more place before I went home. I looked around to be certain no one was watching, then I climbed the fire escape ladder to the top of the nearest building. Pirate Ninja always did his best work from the air.

I worked my way from rooftop to rooftop, making

certain my city was safe, at least for one more night. The last building I needed to check was the First National Bank of Kings Cove. I figured if there was ever going to be a mother of all jobs, a bank heist would be a pretty good candidate.

I jumped to the roof of the bank. First I checked the perimeter of the building, peering over the edges. The number of citizens in the street was steadily decreasing. Not only was there no big job for me to find, there was no Pirate Ninja for *them* to find.

Then I made my way to the center of the bank's roof. I peered down through the skylight.

That's when I heard the voice.

It was raspy, as if someone was trying to disguise their real voice. And it was coming from behind me.

I whirled around.

I couldn't believe it. Before me, incredibly, stood Pirate Ninja. It was *me*. Only bigger. Much bigger.

And *me* was holding a large burlap sack.

"Who are you?" I said. "And what's in the bag?"

"Simple," the raspy-voiced man answered. "I'm Pirate Ninja, and I just stole a lot of money from this bank."

"You're Pirate Ninja?" I said. "I don't think so." I ripped off my ghost costume, pulled out my wooden sword, and prepared my battle stance. "I'm the *real* Pirate Ninja!" I shouted. "What kind of game are you playing?"

He dropped the bag on the roof, pulled out his own sword, and got into a fighting stance. "Game? There's no game. I'm Pirate Ninja, and I just stole a lot of money from the bank. Unfortunately, the whole thing was videotaped. And after I defeat you right now, the whole world will know that *you* are a criminal."

"You're trying to frame me?"

He launched himself at me with incredible speed. I dove to my left and stuck out my sword, but he deftly jumped over it, changed directions, and leapt toward me. His front kick caught me in the thigh and sent me tumbling. I jumped back to my feet, but I was limping.

"Who are you?" I asked.

He cackled in response. "Someone far, far better than Pirate Ninja," he said. "In fact, I'm getting rather tired of this little costume."

He ripped off his Pirate Ninja costume, revealing, underneath it, a solid black ninja costume. It had shiny metal armor that covered his shoulders, chest, elbows, and knees.

"You're a ninja?" I said.

"Not just any ninja," he said. "I am *Double Ninja!*"

"Wait—did you say Double Ninja?"

"Yes!" He cackled again. "I am the great Double Ninja!"

"But that's a terrible name."

"And you, sir, have a terrible face!"

"Um," I said. "That doesn't make any sense."

"Your *face* doesn't make any sense!"

"Come on, dude, I thought my superhero chitchat was bad, but yours is terrible."

Then Double Ninja screamed and came at with a speed I'd never seen before. I dodged his first punch, but not his second. And his spinning back kick caught me right in the stomach. I flew back six feet and landed flat on my back. I could hardly breathe. I tried to get up, but Double Ninja was too fast. He swung his wooden sword at my hands and crushed my knuckles. I screamed. He kicked me in the stomach again, and I lost all my air.

He stood over me, laughing. He held his wooden sword up in the air like he was going to finish me.

I was dizzy and could barely see. He'd beaten me up good. I could barely get my bearings. But then my super vision caught something. Two tiny letters on his neck—a tattoo. It read: *B.K.*

I needed to remember that.

"I'm going to have fun finishing you off," said Double Ninja.

Rolling to one side, I grabbed my sword, and with my last remaining strength, I flung it at him.

The handle hit him square in the face.

He howled in pain.

That gave me just enough time to get to my feet. I put my fists up, but he was way too fast. He leapt at me, ducked under my weak roundhouse, then blasted me with two hard punches to the face that sent me flying to the ground.

After that, everything got dizzy. I felt like I was

going to throw up. I couldn't move, and I could just barely see. I could only watch as Double Ninja opened his big bag and pulled out a smaller bag from it. He placed it near me. Then he lowered himself down beside me and whispered.

"You broke my nose with that stunt. You'll pay for this, Pirate Ninja. But not tonight. Those are my orders. Tonight, you belong to the police. When they see the video, they'll see that Pirate Ninja was behind the robbery. Then they'll find you all alone up on this roof, with some of the stolen money. You'll be in jail... finished. And more than that, you'll be disgraced."

He grabbed a handful of money from the bag and dropped it onto my chest.

"You messed with the Vulture. And it took a Double Ninja to finish you off. Pity. I was hoping you'd put up more of a fight."

Then Double Ninja ran away, and I was all alone on the rooftop.

I tried to move, but the pain was too intense.

My head felt like mush. All I wanted to do was sleep.

I heard the sound of police sirens. They were coming closer.

I figured the next person I saw would be a policeman, gun drawn, handcuffs at the ready. My life would be over. My mom would be crushed.

I would no longer get to eat her beef lasagna on Wednesday nights.

I heard footsteps on the roof, and I gritted my teeth in anticipation of what was about to happen. Then I opened my eyes and saw someone coming toward me.

It wasn't the police.

The figure that approached me was white— but not like a ghost. More like a cat. It moved quickly and gracefully.

I tried to speak, but the figure held a finger up to its mouth.

It picked me up, put my arm over its shoulder, and dragged me toward the edge of the roof.

The sirens were all around now.

"We have to be quick," the figure said. The voice was soft and whispery. "They'll be here soon."

"Who are you?" I somehow managed to ask.

"The White Puma."

"How did you—? Where did you come from?"

"None of that's important. We just need to get you to safety."

We climbed down the fire escape ladder, the White Puma going first. Climbing down that

ladder hurt every bone in my body, and I felt so
dizzy, I wanted to throw up. When I was ten feet
from the ground, my hands slipped, and I fell.
But the White Puma was below me on the
ground, and caught me, the weight of my body
almost sending us both to the ground. I felt
myself being dragged a few feet, and then I was
set down gently on the back of a vehicle.

A motor started, and we began to move. I
went in and out of sleep as the motor chugged
along. Eventually the lights of the city faded. I
could smell the water of Kings Cove and fish and
the docks. The White Puma dragged me out of
what I'd concluded must be some sort of four-
wheeler. I was laid down on the wooden dock.

"You're going to be okay," the White Puma
said in that soft, whispery voice.

I sure didn't feel like I was going to be okay.
But still, I said the only thing I could.

"Thank you."

Then I watched as the White Puma drove away.

I don't know how long I lay there, but at some point, arms grabbed me. Not those of the White Puma. These were big, strong arms. They lifted me up and carried me like I was a sack of potatoes. I was hauled through a familiar room, then back into the area in which I'd trained so much. When I was laid down on the wrestling mats where we did our training, I saw who had been carrying me.

Grievous. He was back!

"Am I dead?" I asked.

Grievous shook his head. "Not quite. No, Archie, you're not dead. But you sure did get hurt."

He examined my face and body.

"What looks the worst?" I said.

He frowned. "Pretty much all of it. But don't worry, I know a few secrets of how to help you heal."

"You do?"

"Yes, Archie, I do. But first, a word of warning." He clapped his hands together and rubbed them together.

"What's that?"

He smiled. "It's gonna hurt."

And you know what? It did hurt. A lot.

But while my bones and muscles ached and screamed, my mind couldn't help but think about what I'd gotten myself into. I was a kid from Nebraska who had found himself the resident superhero of Kings Cove, California, the weirdest town in America.

And that had all been cool, and relatively

harmless... until tonight.

The Vulture had set me up. Had sent someone after me.

Double Ninja.

And if it hadn't been for the equally strange White Puma, I'd be in a jail cell right now.

So as I lay on the mat of our training room that night, I came to a decision. I sat up.

"Archie, lie back down. It's time to rest."

"Commander Grievous," I said, "the Vulture sent a Double Ninja after me tonight, and the people of Kings Cove are at risk. I don't think it's time to rest at all."

"You don't?" he said.

"No." I grabbed one of the wooden training swords and tossed it his way. I staggered to my feet and prepared my battle stance.

"I think it's time to fight!"

Are You Ready For The Next Exciting Project Gemini Book?

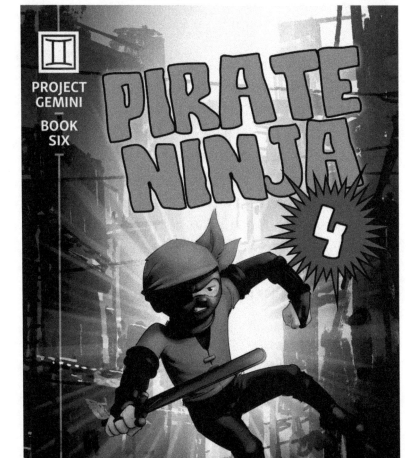

PROJECT
GEMINI

BOOK
SIX

PIRATE NINJA

4

RISE OF THE NIMRODS

DANIEL KENNEY

Supervillains Destroy Thanksgiving!

It's Turkey Day in Kings Cove, California. Archie Beller and his friends are getting their float ready for the town's big parade. Just a nice quiet holiday to enjoy good food with good people. **Wrong!** The Supervillains of Kings Cove are loose and they've got Big Bad Plans! So big that not even a Pirate Ninja can stop them. *And what's worse, someone he loves is in trouble.* This time, Archie will need help. A special kind of help. **He'll need the help of the mighty Nimrods!**

A Word From Daniel Kenney

Thank you for reading *Pirate Ninja 3*, the fifth book in the Project Gemini Series. I hope you enjoyed it.

The sixth Project Gemini book gives us our fourth Pirate Ninja story. In this adventure, Archie and the Nimrods find themselves trying to defend Kings Cove from Supervillains. Will they save the day? Or will this be the end for Archie... and his friends? I hope you give *Pirate Ninja 4* a try and then come back for *Lunchmeat Lenny 1*, which is the seventh book in the Project Gemini series.

Get TWO Daniel Kenney Stories FOR FREE

Building a relationship with my readers is the very best thing about writing. I occasionally send newsletters with details on new releases, special offers and other bits of news relating to Project Gemini and my other books for kids.

And if you sign up to this mailing list I will send you this FREE content:

1. A free copy of my picture book, When Mr. Push Came to Shove.
2. A free copy of my hilarious illustrated book for young people, The Big Life of Remi Muldoon.

You can get both books for free, by signing up at www.DanielKenney.com.

DID YOU ENJOY THIS BOOK? YOU CAN MAKE A BIG DIFFERENCE.

REVIEWS ARE THE MOST POWERFUL TOOL IN MY ARSENAL WHEN IT COMES TO GETTING ATTENTION FOR MY BOOKS. MUCH AS I'D LIKE TO, I AM NOT A BIG NEW YORK PUBLISHER AND I CAN'T TAKE OUT FULL SIZE ADS IN THE NEW YORK TIMES OR GET MYSELF A SPOT ON NATIONAL TELEVISION TALK SHOWS.

BUT **I AM HOPING** THAT I CAN EARN SOMETHING MUCH MORE POWERFUL THAN THOSE THINGS. SOMETHING THE BIG PUBLISHERS WOULD LOVE TO HAVE.

A COMMITTED AND LOYAL BUNCH OF READERS.

HONEST REVIEWS OF MY BOOKS HELP BRING THEM TO THE ATTENTION OF OTHER READERS. IF YOU'VE ENJOYED THIS BOOK, I'D BE VERY GRATEFUL IF YOU COULD SPEND JUST FIVE MINUTES LEAVING A REVIEW (IT CAN BE AS SHORT AS YOU LIKE) ON THE BOOK'S AMAZON PAGE.

THANK YOU VERY MUCH!

Project Gemini Books

Book One: Pirate Ninja 1
Book Two: Lovable Loser 1
Book Three: Pirate Ninja 2
Book Four: Lovable Loser 2
Book Five: Pirate Ninja 3
Book Six: Pirate Ninja 4
Book Seven: Lunchmeat Lenny 1
Book Eight: Lunchmeat Lenny 2
Book Nine: The Unbeatable Olive Klein
Book Ten: Gemini Squad

Also By Daniel Kenney

The Math Inspectors Series
The Science Inspectors Series
The History Mystery Kids Series
The Big Life of Remi Muldoon Series
Teenage Treasure Hunter
Katie Plumb & The Pendleton Gang
But, I Still Had Feet

✺ PROJECT GEMINI BOOKS

BOOK ONE

BOOK TWO

BOOK THREE

BOOK FOUR

BOOK FIVE

BOOK SIX

BOOK SEVEN

BOOK EIGHT

BOOK NINE

BOOK TEN

ABOUT THE AUTHOR

Daniel Kenney is the author of the breakout hit The Math Inspectors and the fantastic series for reluctant readers, Project Gemini. He is also the author of the popular Science Inspectors, History Mystery Kids, and The Big Life of Remi Muldoon.

He makes his online home at www.DanielKenney.com.

You can connect with Daniel at www.facebook.com/AuthorDanielKenney and if you have any questions, please email him at DanielKenneyBooks@gmail.com.

CPSIA information can be obtained
at www.ICGtesting.com
Printed in the USA
LVHW03s2024210618
581511LV00002B/338/P